A
atheneum

ATHENEUM BOOKS FOR YOUNG READERS
An imprint of Simon & Schuster Children's Publishing Division
1230 Avenue of the Americas, New York, New York 10020
Text copyright © 2015 by George Ella Lyon and Benn Lyon
Illustrations copyright © 2015 by Mick Wiggins
All rights reserved, including the right of reproduction in whole or in part in any form.
ATHENEUM BOOKS FOR YOUNG READERS is a registered trademark of Simon & Schuster, Inc.
Atheneum logo is a trademark of Simon & Schuster, Inc.
For information about special discounts for bulk purchases, please contact Simon & Schuster Special Sales at 1-866-506-1949 or business@simonandschuster.com.
The Simon & Schuster Speakers Bureau can bring authors to your live event. For more information or to book an event, contact the Simon & Schuster Speakers Bureau at 1-866-248-3049 or visit our website at www.simonspeakers.com.
Book design by Debra Sfetsios-Conover
The text for this book is set in Rockwell.
The illustrations for this book are rendered digitally.
Manufactured in China
0615 SCP
First Edition
1 2 3 4 5 6 7 8 9 10
Library of Congress Cataloging-in-Publication Data
Lyon, George Ella, 1949– author.
Boats float! / George Ella Lyon and Benn Lyon ; illustrated by Mick Wiggins.—
First edition.
pages cm
"A Richard Jackson Book."
Summary: In rhyming text the reader is introduced to all the different kinds of boats floating on rivers, lakes, oceans, and ponds.
ISBN 978-1-4814-0380-1 (hardcover)
ISBN 978-1-4814-0381-8 (eBook)
1. Boats and boating—Juvenile fiction. 2. Stories in rhyme. [1. Stories in rhyme. 2. Boats and boating—Fiction.] I. Lyon, Benn, author. II. Wiggins, Mick, illustrator. III. Title.
PZ8.3.L9893Bo 2015
[E]—dc23
2014034649

For Dick Jackson
an ocean of love & thanks
for all our voyages
—G. E. L.

For Cheryl Wurtele
Best Boss
—B. G. L.

To Honey and Maggie, and everyone else in
our fine little boat.
—M. W.

BOATS FLOAT!

By George Ella Lyon and Benn Lyon

Illustrations by Mick Wiggins

 A Richard Jackson Book

atheneum ATHENEUM BOOKS FOR YOUNG READERS   NEW YORK   LONDON   TORONTO   SYDNEY   NEW DELHI

Boats have keels.
Boats have hulls
lifted by waves,
followed by gulls.

Boats float!

Motorboats,
rowboats,
cabins-down-below boats.

Sailboats,
mail boats,
waving-from-the-rail boats.

Bow and stern,
bilge and beam—
from fore to aft
boats ride the stream.

Sails and engines,
paddles and oars
make the trip
from shore to shore.

Boats float!

Who's in charge
of that large barge?

Captain at the wheel,
first mate on the deck,
crew on every level
check what must be checked.

A lookout's on the *poop deck*.
Controls are on the *bridge*.
The bathroom's called the *head*.
The *galley* holds the fridge.

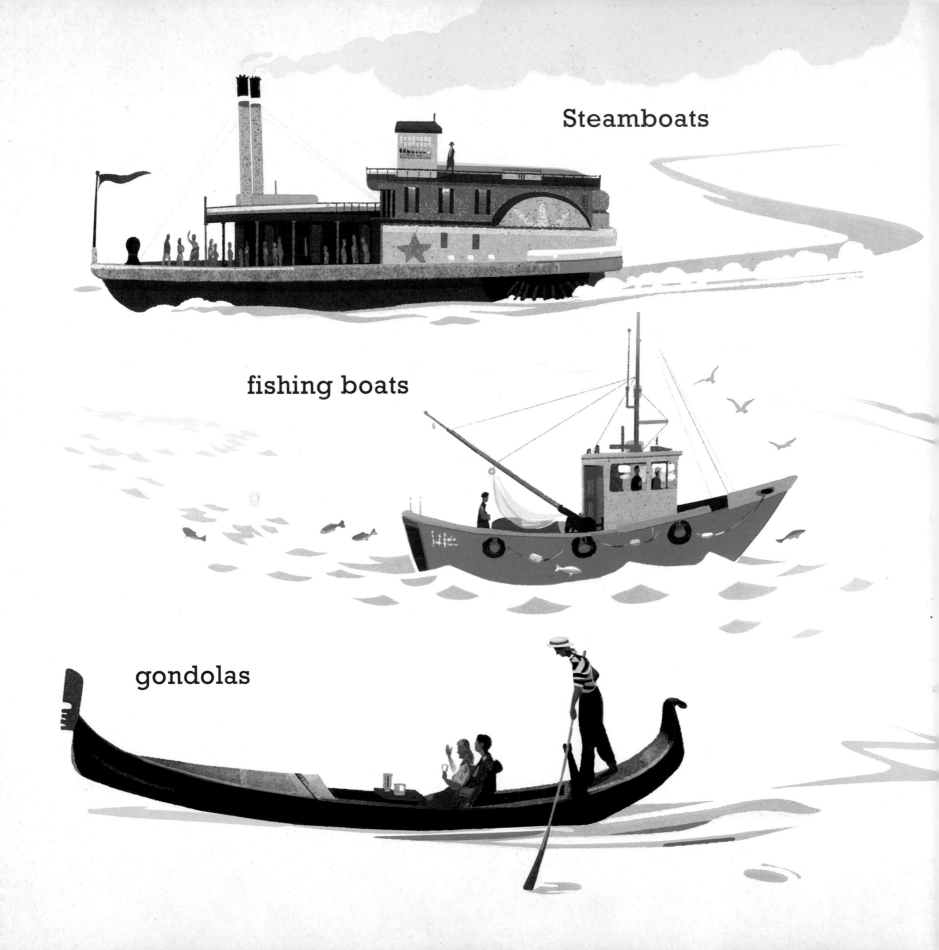

Steamboats

fishing boats

gondolas

skiffs

banana boats

bilibilis

Ghost ships adrift . . .

Boats float!

When seaplanes land
they land on floats,
so on the water
seaplanes are boats.

If a boat can dive
and travel unseen
beneath the waves,
it's a submarine.

Houseboats, sloops, river wherries; car, train, and people ferries.

Pirate ships, sampans, junks, canoes.
So many boats! How can you choose?

Boats boats boats boats float float float float.

Want a small boat?
A not-very-tall boat?

Try coracles, dinghies, bathtubs, rafts—
so short that fore is almost aft.

The smallest boats are ships in bottles.
But they don't sail. They're just models.

Toy boats, bath boats,
scrub and rub-a-dub boats.

Want a grand boat?
A travel-far-from-land boat?

Board an ocean liner.
Voyage for a week.
Climb from deck to deck
to find what you seek:
bowling alley, movies,
ice cream, books,
and the million-colored ocean
everywhere you look.

If the day is blazing
and you want to get cool,
jump right into
the ship's swimming pool.

And if you stretch out and float,
you'll be acting like a boat!

Boats float!